Edgar Allan

Edgar Allan

by John Neufeld   S. G. Phillips, New York

Copyright © 1968 by S.G. Phillips, Inc.
Library of Congress Catalog Card Number 68-31175
Designed by David Miller
Manufactured in the United States of America

FOURTH PRINTING, 1971

for Twink,
as a promise

Edgar Allan

1

This is a story about my father, and about God. Neither is very easy to understand.

My father, the Reverend Robert Fickett, is a very tall, very straight man, who looks like what King Charles II must have looked like when he grew older and stopped tearing around the countryside of old England. You can tell he's had a lot of fun by the lines around his eyes.

Father has a sense of humor, but he can be serious when he has to be. And he can scare you sometimes if you're listening to him during the sermon.

He and I used to do a lot of walking together, and he would do most of the talking. Father would say that each man is made of small parts that fit together to make a "whole" man. A "whole man," Father said, could not divide his life into parts that were lived differently

What this means, I guess, for me, is that going to school, playing around, doing chores, and everything else I do is part of the same thing. For Father, it would be his church and his family and his life that have all to be lived in the same way.

When Father talked like this, I mostly listened. It would have been easier if he had told me to be honest, or thrifty, or kind. But Father thought he should treat each of us as though we were as old as he, which meant that he talked to us as though we could all understand him. Sometimes he would leave things out for us to figure out later; sometimes he would use words that made you want to go look up every other one in the dictionary.

About God I can't say too much. No one can, I guess. But He's important in our family, and not just because Father is a minister.

My mother, who is tall, too, and gray, likes to say that God is everywhere, and you can only hope to understand Him by seeing where He is and where He *isn't*. She thinks that where He isn't is often more interesting, and tells us more about Him and His ways, than where He is.

Actually, my mother isn't any easier to understand than my father.

It was last summer when all this began. There were seven of us Ficketts then, including my parents. First, there was my older sister, Mary Nell. We call her M.N. unless we're mad at her. She was fourteen then, and impossible. I didn't like her much, but maybe I was being too rough. I've been told I'm a harsh judge sometimes.

She had a problem, Mary Nell. She didn't like being a minister's daughter. She could be mean about it, too. I suppose it's because she felt her life had been ruined or something. I never felt that way.

My name is Michael, plain and simple, and I'm twelve now. I'm the only child in our family without a middle name.

The reason I never felt the same way M.N. did is that, while being a minister's kid isn't always fun, it does mean you get to do things pretty much on your own. You *have* to, because other kids never let you forget who you are, or what you're supposed to be. I mean, to them you're something very goody-goody. You can spend a lot of time trying to prove you're not.

So, I spend a lot of *my* time alone. That doesn't mean I'm a hermit. I just don't always care for other kids, is all. The only way I could ever be part of a gang would be by proving I'm really O.K. (which I really am) and to do the kinds of things I've been told not to. I guess I never feel that mean towards my father.

I mean, take the way kids sometimes steal things. Nothing very big or anything, but just taking little things from shops for the fun of trying to get away with it.

Once, I think when I was ten, I went into a stationery-store with some guys in my class. One of them started talking to the old man behind the counter, and asked him for something. Envelopes, I think. Anyway, when the man bent down beneath the counter to get what we had asked for, four hands shot up and grabbed everything they could get a grip on. It was sort of funny.

So I smiled and watched. But I didn't take anything.

Now, you wouldn't think that not taking something would be the worst thing that ever happened. But to these guys it was. I might as well not even have been there, they said, if I wasn't going to be part of them. I said I was, and they said how could I be when I couldn't stop thinking dumb thoughts about right and wrong? After all, they should have known, me being a minister's kid and everything.

I told my father about this. He said that sometimes it takes more courage to say "no" than to say "yes." I thought about that a while, and then forgot about it. I was maybe ten, then.

So what I do a lot now, instead of not stealing, is read. I'm sort of a nut on history. English history. I know some things I'll never even be able to remember. This is mostly because I'll probably never need to remember them.

After me comes Sally Ann, who is, now, nearly six. Sally Ann stands for "Seven a.m.," which is when she was born. "M.N.," Mary Nell, means "mid-night." My mother thought of all this.

I have hopes for Sally Ann. She's smart and patient, and sort of scary about everything. She sees more of things than I do, and, if she could, she'd probably write all this down a lot better than I will. Because, though I try to remember as much as I can, there were a lot of other things going on in my life besides just this one thing, and I know I'll forget some of them. Sally Ann never would.

Which is to say, I sometimes think Sally Ann does have eyes in the back of her head, and I envy her. Anyway, she's my favorite. Tiny, and bright-eyed, and funny because she doesn't yet know how she looks to other people.

Next to last was Stephen Paul. Naturally, that's "Seven p.m." He's almost four now.

There's not much to be said for Stephen. It's too early. So far, though, he's O.K., and he doesn't give anyone except Sally Ann any trouble. And that's only because she insists on trying to teach him things. I don't think Stephen cares a lot about learning.

Last came Edgar Allan. "E.A." for Early Afternoon. He was the youngest and was sort of, well, cute. He was black.

2

It doesn't say much, the word "cute." But that's all you could say about him when we got him. He was.

The funny thing was we didn't know he was coming. Of course, it was last summer then, so maybe if he arrived today we would be smarter. I'm not certain.

We *had* heard some talk. Or really, what we heard was parts of talks between my parents. Our house, which is fairly big, has a study for Father off the living-room, and that's where he and Mother have their serious talks. Because the study is so close to where we sometimes are, we can often hear what they're saying.

Mary Nell heard it first. She came to me, and we tried to guess what the few things she had overheard could mean. (M.N. probably eavesdropped. She was like that.)

We didn't have much to go on. "It would be good for the other children," was one sentence she heard, but that could have meant almost anything. "The most important thing we could do," was another bit, just as puzzling.

"It won't be easy, especially later," my mother had said. "A probation period" meant nothing to M.N. or to me. "We'll cross those bridges when we get to them," Father said once. To which Mother replied, "I think we ought to cross them now." M.N. and I were very confused.

"Not just for us, but for the community and the church," was the last thing M.N. had caught, from Father. And then we heard nothing until dinner one night a few weeks later.

It was right after Stephen Paul's third birthday, and he was sitting at the table in a regular chair for the first time. It was a sort of graduation dinner, and Stephen's high-chair was in the corner to remind him, I guess, that he was now "grown up." Sally Ann had been coaching him all day on his table manners, but Stephen sat at the table playing with his food and looking around and ignoring all Sally Ann's instructions. I suspect Stephen had been over-rehearsed.

"We're going to have a newcomer here at dinner soon," Mother said.

"Oh?" said M.N., not paying much attention. "Who?"

"Your new brother," answered my mother.

M.N. heard *this*. So did we all, S.A. and me. We just stared at her.

"But Mother!" M.N. said. "You couldn't have been . . . all this time without our knowing . . . I mean. . . !"

"M.N., what your mother means is that we are thinking of adopting a little boy," Father said quickly. "We thought you might want to know in advance."

"Having another child doesn't mean any less attention for you children, or less love, you know," Mother said to Sally Ann. "It just means that we have so much, your father and I, that we thought we could surely spare some for one more child."

There was a pause, and then M.N. jumped right in. "Well," she said, "I think it's just marvey. It's so much easier this way, isn't it, Mother?"

My mother laughed. "In some ways."

"Four seems like a pretty good family," I said. No one paid any attention.

"How old is he?" S.A. wanted to know. "Will I be able to play with him?"

"He's younger than you are, dear," answered Mother. "He would be younger, even, than Stephen."

"Good," S.A. said. "Then I can take care of him, too."

"There is one thing," Mother started to say, "that I think you ought to —"

But Father interrupted. "Yes," he said. "We wondered if you by chance had any preferences . . . like the color of his eyes, or hair or skin, or shoe size. Details like that."

"Just as long as he can learn things," S.A. said.

"It's rather more serious than that," Mother began again. "We have told the adoption agency that we would be glad to have a child who was . . . different. A little boy who might be Chinese, or Negro, or Mexican. Some one who might need help and a family like ours more than other children."

"You mean you don't actually know what you're getting?" M.N. asked suddenly.

"Well," Father said, "we think we do. But we're not certain, really, are we, dear?"

"No," Mother said. "We're just hoping."

"But when he gets here," Father said, "and while he *will* be living with us, he won't really be *ours* for nearly a year."

"Why is that?" I asked. "Whose idea is that?"

"It's the way an adoption agency works," Father explained. "They want to be sure their children are happy in their new homes, and so they put everyone on a sort of test. At the end of the test, if all goes well, then they are happy enough to lose their children because they know the children themselves are happy."

"That's reasonable," M.N. said sharply. "You never know. You could make a mistake."

"Yes, that's true," admitted Father. "So we all have to be extra careful and on our best behavior for a while. I know you won't disappoint your mother or me."

"*I* won't," S.A. said.

"When he arrives, your new brother," said Mother, "if anything occurs to you, or you want to talk about him, please just promise you'll come to your father or me first. Try not to upset *him*. He'll be too young to understand, of course, but some children learn to hear well before they learn to speak. None of us would want to say anything that might make him unhappy."

"I don't see how we could," M.N. said. "After all, he's only a child."

My father smiled. "Yes, that's true. He's only a child."

"I just hope he can learn things," Sally Ann said to Mother as they both began to clear the table.

3

Edgar Allan arrived about two weeks later, right on schedule: Early in the Afternoon. And he was cute.

Sally Ann went out of her head for him right from the start. Here was *another* pupil, nearly three years old, with enormous brown eyes in a clean, dark, shiny face, with the sort of giggle that made you giggle back.

When I walked in, Edgar Allan, Stephen, and S.A. were all on the floor, on hands and knees, "learning." S.A. was "reading" to them from a picture book.

I think I just stood there a minute. I was surprised. That was all. Just surprised. Maybe I never really expected exactly what we got.

The first thing I noticed, after I stopped being surprised, was that Edgar Allan and Stephen gave S.A. the same amount of attention and interest as far as learning things went. That means, not a lot. They were too busy with other things, like just crawling around.

"Well?" my father said to me.

"Well!" I said back, and though I don't know why, I smiled.

He smiled, too, and nodded. "I thought so," he said.

"What?"

"That you wouldn't say anything right away."

"I don't know what to say," I answered. "I like to think first, sometimes."

I turned back and passed the three children on the floor, sort of sinking into a chair at the end of the room so I could watch them.

E.A. was so cute you wouldn't believe it. I think he was the cutest kid I ever saw in my life. Much more than Stephen Paul ever was, for example. *He* looked just like any other little kid you've ever seen.

You couldn't tell much else about Edgar Allan. He was a little slow, I guess, in learning how to talk, and you never knew whether he was listening to you or not. He certainly didn't give you much to work with.

So I just sat there a while, watching. And I was still there when M.N. came home.

She walked in the door, turned towards where the noise was rising every minute, and stepped into the room.

She stood there. Her mouth opened. Her face reddened. And then she walked out. Just like that.

"Mary Nell!" called my mother. But M.N. didn't answer. She ran up the stairs to her room, and we didn't see her until dinner.

4

Dinner wasn't much fun, for four of us. M.N. wouldn't say a word. She wouldn't look at Edgar Allan, who had Stephen's old high-chair now. And she ate hardly anything on her plate.

Mother tried to get her to talk about what she'd done during the day. And Father tried to help. But M.N. just sat there.

I wasn't sure what to do, so I didn't do anything. I watched M.N. part of the time, and Sally Ann, who was diligently teaching E.A. the difference between a fork and a spoon, part of the time, and wondered, sort of.

When dinner was over, though, Mary Nell finally spoke.

"You asked us, Mother, to talk to you and father first about him. Well, I want to. Tonight."

M.N.'s voice seemed very old to me suddenly.

"All right, Mary Nell," said Mother. "We'll meet you in the study as soon as we put everyone to bed."

"Fine," said M.N., and pushed her chair away from the table. Without even offering to help clear, she left the room.

I looked at Father.

"Michael," he said, "I've tried to teach you all to think first and speak later. I thought M.N. had never learned that lesson as well as you. But I was wrong."

"What are you going to do?" I asked.

"Listen to Mary Nell," said Father. "Listen, and try to help."

"I don't think it's help she wants to talk about," I said.

"No, I don't think so, either," said Father.

5

As it turned out, it wasn't Father at all Mary Nell wanted to talk to. What made the whole thing a woman's problem I don't know, but Father was ushered out, not very politely, and could only turn towards the study door as it was closed in his face to say, "We'll be in here if you need us."

He was very quiet as he joined me in front of the television set.

We sat there a moment, and then we both realized the same thing at the same time. We could hear everything Mary Nell and Mother said anyway, right through the noise of the set. I was sort of glad, I admit, but I don't think Father was.

So, in between "Coral Canyon," which isn't my favorite show anyway, we had "Mother and Mary Nell."

"I just don't see how you could do it," M.N. was saying. "A Chinese, or a Mexican, or anything else. But not this! Without even asking us, Mother!"

"Mary Nell, your father and I don't *have* to ask you children about everything. Some things we do because we know and feel they are right and best for the family. If we're wrong, then we have ourselves to blame. If we're right, we try very hard not to say I told you so."

"Marvey! Just *mar*vey! That's worked before. But this is different, for Pete's sake! This is different. At least you could have told us as soon as you knew. I mean, *really* told us, Michael and me. We're certainly old enough to be told."

I gave M.N. five mental points for that. I agreed.

"What would you have said, M.N.?" asked Mother.

"Well, *I* don't know. *Something.* At least we would have known exactly what to expect."

"Why is that so important? Should your feelings be any different?"

"That's not the point, Mother," said M.N. rather sharply. "We would have had time to think, and to make up our minds what our feelings were going to be."

"Sally Ann and Stephen had no more warning than you, dear. Their feelings seem to be just as real as yours, and rather nicer."

"You think I'm prejudiced, is that all?" M.N. asked, pretty close to tears. (I could tell, even through the door.)

"What would you say you were, M.N.?"

"Well, *honest,* anyway! Have you or Father even once stopped to think what will happen when he grows up? Can you imagine the look on my friends' faces when I introduce him as my *brother*? Don't you know what they're going to think to themselves, about *you*?"

It was quiet then, for a moment. I think Mother was a little surprised. I know I was. But M.N. went on fast. Once she has the advantage, she never loses it.

"It's not enough that we're your kids, is it? That we have to prove that minister's kids can be O.K. just like anyone else's? You have to give us something else to struggle with!"

"Mary Nell," said Mother sort of slowly, "I don't think you've given Edgar Allan an honest chan—"

"Mother, I am giving him the exact same chance he's going to get with everyone else in this town. He *is* black! It's that easy. He's visible, and he's different, and he *is not ours*! Michael and I have a bad enough time, but think what this will do to Stephen. They're both about the same age. They'll always just be two odd-balls together. Is that fair?"

"Mary Nell!" Mother finally was mad.

"What?" Mary Nell shouted right back.

There was an awful long pause.

"Mary Nell," said Mother more quietly. "Edgar Allan is going to grow up here with us. He will have the same advantages and the same disadvantages all of you have. Your father and I thought we had a family wise enough and confident enough to be able to face the problems that frighten you so. Perhaps we were wrong. Still, we are determined to give something to E.A. And I suspect that by doing so, we can even give *you* something."

"What, besides more problems?"

"Integrity," Mother said. "It's a lonesome gift, I admit. But it's a valuable one, nevertheless."

"Swell," said M.N. "That's just swell! Thanks a lot!" And then she just walked out of the study and up to her room.

Father suddenly leaned forward, pretending to be fascinated by "Coral Canyon," as Mother stood in the doorway to the study.

6

About two minutes later, Father and I left the house for a walk.

It was still light enough so you could *see* mosquitoes rather than just hear them too late. And it was the first walk of ours I could remember when Father didn't start right out talking.

We walked sort of slowly. His hands were in his pockets; mine were behind me like Prince Philip's always are. After a while, when I realized that Father just wanted company, not talk, I began playing Prince Philip, sort of nodding to people who weren't there as we walked the length of the longest throne-room in the world.

After a while, I stopped imagining I was in Buckingham Palace, and paid more attention to where I really was.

Our town is a funny sort of place. Where we live, the houses are enormous. There are lots of Spanish-type houses, with red tile roofs, and with doorways that open onto little courts planted with cactus and ice-plants and ivy. There are some houses that remind me of Norman castles in books, and some that are sort of nothing houses, just big and dark.

The streets are mostly evenly planted with big palms, and there are eucalyptus trees every once in a while, set back from the roads. These, and the flowers, combine at night to make the air so heavy with smells and so sweet you get sort of dizzy. I like it. It's certainly better air than we used to have in Cleveland.

And we're not far from the ocean either, which is sensational. Father says I'm still too young to begin surfing, but whenever that day finally comes, I think I'll probably leave home forever and just surf my way around the world.

One of the nice things about where we live is that our house isn't right next door to the church. It was that way in Cleveland, and it used to depress me sometimes. That was before I discovered English history, though, and before I learned how to organize life, sort of. It wouldn't bother me so much now. Still, it was bleak waking up each morning, and going to bed each night, with a steeple staring you in the face.

One good thing about Father, though, is that he never quotes the Bible. Or almost never. He saves this for sermons, or for Sunday School, or maybe, once in a while, for his classes at the school our church runs.

Actually, it seems to me that Father does pretty much what any other father does, except, of course, on Sundays. I mean, he gets up each day and leaves the house just like anyone else, and doesn't come back until late afternoon. He visits people who belong to our church, or teaches history at the school (where he's also the principal), or sometimes works on committees around town that are always doing something good. And although most kids don't have to sit still, and awake, and listen to their fathers talk about good and evil, and what to do and what not to do, every Sunday morning at eleven a.m. sharp, it really doesn't do any harm.

I don't go to the church school, and neither does M.N. Actually, the church school isn't just for the kids of people who belong to our church. It's for anyone who can get in, I guess, and who can pay tuition, but it's sponsored by the church. Really, it's just a small sort of private school, and since M.N. and I had gone to the public schools in Cleveland, Mother decided we should keep at it. Sally Ann and Stephen could go to the church school when they were old enough, she said, but she thought we would learn more of the world, I guess, if we were in a larger part of it, rather than in a small exclusive part.

I'm glad, because you can have more fun in regular school than in a private one. Still, when I do something that displeases Father, he liked to scare me by threatening to send me away to a military academy, which is a private school times two, so it would be twice as bad.

He never would, of course. Send me away.

Because, really, though we get tangled up sometimes trying to say what we mean, we do sort of communicate pretty well. And we find there are a lot of things we like together. From peanut-butter and sweet pickle sandwiches, to tennis and swimming, to English history. And a lot of stuff in between.

Anyway, as I started to say a while back, our town is a funny sort of place. Because it's not really very real, if you know what I mean. Most towns have tall buildings and rivers and a baseball team. Ours has no skyscrapers, the ocean instead, and we have to cheer for San Francisco if we want to cheer at all.

Also, most towns have all sorts of people. Our town doesn't. I mean, they don't *live* here. There's no rule about it, I guess, but they just don't.

We do have some people who come to our town to work, though. We have Negroes, and Mexicans, and I once saw a Japanese man who was working in someone's garden. But I don't think any of these people really have houses and families and television sets and lawns of their own to cut right here in town.

Which, I suppose, (all of this, that is) makes us sort of special. Some people would say "better" instead, but I'm not exactly sure it is. It's just different, is all, and not very real — certainly not much like Cleveland where we had everyone in the world doing something.

But it is a nice place to live, and I like it much, much better than I did dull old Ohio with its snow and wind and ice in winter, and its dead heat in the summer.

So, I guess we were pretty lucky, right about up to the very minute that Edgar Allan arrived.

"What are you thinking so deeply about, Michael?" Father asked me suddenly.

"I was thinking about Edgar Allan," I said.

"What about him?"

"Why *didn't* you tell M.N. and me about him? I mean, that we were really going to get a Negro? I thought you always wanted us to know everything."

"Well," Father said, "when we mentioned it, your mother and I weren't really certain we would get him. We had asked for a Negro child, but we just couldn't be sure."

"Oh," I said. "Do you think M.N. would have been so mad if you'd gotten someone different?"

"Who can say?" Father said. "We suspected, your mother and I, that of all the children, if we had any difficulty at all it would be from M.N. I suppose it might have been easier for her had we gotten someone else."

"What does Mother think of all this?" I asked.

"About what? M.N. or E.A.?"

"Well," I said, "she's stuck with M.N. What does she think about Edgar Allan?"

"She's delighted with him. I'm sure she is."

"But how can you be sure of *anything* like this?"

"Well, I just have that feeling, Michael. Just like the feeling I have about adopting Edgar Allan in the first place. Our family is big enough, and so is our town, to do this. And if they aren't, why then they ought to be."

"Is Mother as certain of all this as you are?" I asked again.

"Oh, Michael," Father laughed. "You know your mother. She's a worrier from way back."

"What do you mean?"

"I love her more than I can ever say, but sometimes I think she thinks too much, Michael. She wants to think, and consider everything first. I want to act instead, and act now."

"Oh," I said. I couldn't think of much more to say.

Actually, the more I thought about it, the more I guessed I was like my mother. I mean, if you can see things coming, you might as well be prepared for them, rather than just let them take you unaware.

Still, we've always been pretty lucky, so I decided not to say anything more, at least right then, to Father.

The thing is, that night for the first time, I got a feeling in my stomach of something about to happen that I wouldn't like very much. I couldn't have told you what it was exactly, but I felt sort of jumpy, and as we turned back towards home I half-expected to see Mary Nell sneaking out of the house with Edgar Allan in a burlap sack, slipping into the bushes, and making a dash to the ocean. Sort of like drowning kittens.

7

Of course, nothing like that happened. When we got home, the three younger kids were sound asleep, M.N. was in her room doing something secret behind her closed door, and Mother was reading with a cup of coffee at hand. The only sign of our new arrival was the high-chair in the corner of the dining-room, since it had been brought up from the basement for another turn.

We all got over that first day. I often wished I could have asked E.A. what *he* thought about his first day of life at our house, but of course he wouldn't have remembered anything, even if he could have talked.

So the next few weeks passed by. I forgot about the feeling in the pit of my stomach for a while, and we just lived the ordinary way. Except that we all came to know a little more about Edgar Allan.

All of us, that is, except M.N. *She* wouldn't play with him, or look at him at dinner, or even speak to him. She never said "good morning" or "good night" or even her all-purpose word, "marvey." M.N. sort of drew her arms up and around herself and refused to touch anything that had to do with E.A.

But the rest of us learned more about him. "Learned" isn't the right word, exactly. Because, for example, he and Stephen just grew together by growing up together. It was natural and easy. Everything Stephen did, E.A. tried to do. And though none of us could have told you exactly when

Stephen first said anything, or what exactly it was, we all knew precisely when E.A. spoke and what it was he said for that first time.

I think if E.A. and Stephen had been exactly the same age, I would have bet on E.A. to speak first. It was funny, but E.A. just *looked* smarter. Something about how bright his eyes were, and how big a smile he had, I guess. I admit Stephen was at a slight disadvantage because E.A.'s eyes just naturally shone brighter since they were set in darker skin. Still and all, if I'd had to, I would have bet E.A. was just a little smarter.

Anyway, all of us could have told you what it was E.A. said first, when he began speaking at all. Especially M.N.

She, you see, has a few bad speech habits. She uses a word again and again, until you get so tired of hearing it you want to take the word out of her mind and scrub it until it shrinks. Later, you can stick it back in her mind way behind every other word she's ever learned, and wait for it to work itself forward again naturally.

She's always saying "super" for one. It comes out "Sooper!" most of the time. This is supposed to mean something good, obviously. Another thing she says a lot is "just lovely." This always comes out sort of soft and "woman-y" which I guess *she* thinks is sexy. I think it's sickening.

But what she used to say most of the time was "marvey!" This came out "Marrrvee!" and meant pretty much what "Sooper!" did, though it seemed to apply to a lot more things.

Anyhow, there we all were one night at dinner. Mother sat between Stephen and E.A., helping first this one and then that with his food. Actually, E.A. was learning to feed himself at the time, and occasionally he would sort of forget that a spoon was there to help. Lots of fingers, and little piles of food around his chair. Kids are like that.

Naturally, Sally Ann sat on the other side of Edgar Allan, helping him, too, and talking to him all the time.

This, of course, would make all of us laugh, too. We never really got to finish even one book about Winnie and his friends, because Father had his favorite stories and those were all we ever heard. (Except one night, when I found *King John's Christmas* in another book. Father read this aloud, too, in a great English accent, and it became *my* favorite. But that was only once.)

M.N. would still have none of this. She busied herself doing a lot of dumb things that really weren't very important but that kept her apart from us and E.A. Once in a while she would join a picnic, or a trip to the beach, or the one overnight camping trip we took in the mountains.

The thing about M.N. was that if her friends said it was raining, and M.N. was *standing* in the sunshine, she would have agreed, finally, that it was indeed raining. She wanted that much to be part of the crowd. Being M.N. wasn't enough. She had to be Snooty and Fats and everyone else, just so no one would know she was, really, the minister's daughter. M.N. had this problem, and she just couldn't solve it yet.

The rest of us banded together that summer. It was a natural thing to do, because funny things started to happen. After all, you couldn't keep Edgar Allan hidden away from the whole world. And while we have a hedge that runs almost the length of our frontyard, you can see through even that in some places.

The funny things were nothing you could get upset about, really. But every once in a while a crazy kind of look from people in a passing car, or a little extra room around our blankets at the beach. That sort of thing. I guess people were just startled by seeing the five of us playing with the one of E.A., and behaving as though we all belonged together.

It was one thing to see Sally Ann and Stephen, who were just two little kids anywhere, playing with E.A., who just happened to be another little kid. It was something else to watch as E.A. ran to Mother with a skinned knee, or sand in his eyes, or just for hugging.

Anyway, the weather was good and the days were long and filled with fun, as summer ended. It was nearly time for school. M.N. started shopping for all the junk she said she just *had* to have. Sally Ann, who was going to kindergarten, couldn't stand the excitement. She had to know everything in advance, and you could tell she would drive her teacher nuts in a very few weeks. Sally Ann really should always be the teacher herself.

I had passed into sixth grade without too much trouble, and during the summer had discovered I really was a pretty good swimmer. Good enough to make a kind of team that was formed at the beach. I met a lot of new guys there, and I began to have the feeling that maybe some time I wouldn't have to worry about trying to be like everybody else.

It's a funny thing. After I discovered English history, I found myself sort of surrounded by friends. It always feels, when I lie on my bed and read about John and Richard III and Cromwell (the Cardinal, not the Puritan) and others, that really I'm more at home in the streets of ancient London and along its river than I am in our own town. I guess maybe because I rely on these people to keep me company when I'm low, or when things don't seem to be going too well.

But when I got on the swimming team, I don't think more than maybe two people asked me about my family. Either everyone knew I was the minister's kid, or fewer cared. I meant to ask M.N. if she felt this was true in her life, too, but I never got around to doing it. M.N. would probably have said something stupid, or repeated something she had heard from Fats or Snooty. She was like that.

The thing was, M.N. was sort of confused that summer. Sometimes she would be quiet for days, and sometimes you couldn't shut her up. Sometimes she would be as nice as could be, and other times she flew off the handle in seconds. Mother said this had to do with physical things, and I decided it was best to just forget about all *that*, and wait M.N. out. I certainly didn't care why M.N. was agreeable when she was, and I could ditch her when she wasn't. And since you never knew what kind of day M.N. was having until it was too late, I decided just not to talk too much to her for a while.

And so, summer was nearly over. Father didn't yet have to go to school every day. He spent most of his time talking to people around town about different projects, or working on his sermons and reading, or visiting people who belonged to our church.

Sometimes, of course, people visited us.

One Saturday morning, while Mother was out shopping, some ladies from one of the church groups stopped by. I don't think they were expected or anything, but were just out walking and decided to sort of snoop around.

The doorbell rang and S.A. let them in, saying that Mother wasn't home. Then she went to get Father, who was working in his study.

He came out and offered the four ladies coffee, and took them into the kitchen, which is big enough for people just standing around talking. I was finishing a book about the Wars of the Roses in the living-room, so I could sort of hear everything when things began to get interesting.

What happened was that one of the ladies looked out into the backyard and saw E.A. playing with Stephen. "Oh," she said, "isn't that sweet!"

"What's that?" Father wanted to know.

"Why, that little colored boy out there, playing with the other child," the woman said. "He must belong to one of the servants in the neighborhood."

"Not exactly," said Father, "unless of course you mean a servant of the Church."

One lady gasped. (I don't know why; she must have known anyway.) Then Father went on. "It's nothing to be alarmed about, ladies," he said. "The little white boy is my son Stephen. The little colored boy, as you say, is Edgar Allan, a child we have taken in for a while to start out properly."

There was a funny sighing sound. I was a little confused, but I thought maybe Father was breaking it gently to them, about E.A. being ours and everything.

"Is he an orphan, then?" said the woman who had spotted E.A. first.

"Yes, he is," Father answered.

"Ohhh," said the woman again. "Then *I* think it's just wonderfully noble of you both to devote yourselves to his bringing up like this. How marvelous to take him in and give him the advantages of living here a while, before he sees how horrible the rest of the world is."

"Perhaps," said Father slowly, "the world will change, in time. It is a possibility, isn't it?"

And then the subject changed. I think, if I remember, it was Father who changed it. I stopped listening.

I was sort of uneasy, and that feeling that I mentioned before, in my stomach, woke up again and said "Here I am, still," and I didn't really know why. I guess maybe I'm just naturally nervous, or something.

Anyway, that was what our summer was like. Father and I went on our walks, just like before, and he did most of the talking as he had always done. We didn't talk much about E.A. I guess Father expected all of us to treat him the same way we treated each other. Which we did. Except for M.N., still, who would have nothing to do with him.

That was the one thing we *never* talked about on our walks: M.N. Father was hoping that, all by herself, M.N. would change her mind about E.A.

I think Father hoped M.N. would change in what she did rather than ever say anything out loud about it. You could tell it was important for Father from just watching him watch M.N. all the time. Maybe he thought he had done something wrong to wind up with a daughter who disagreed so with what he was doing. But although he once tried to talk to M.N. about it (and she just walked away from him), he never afterwards changed his way or the things he said to her, thinking, I suppose, that the best thing to do was to pretend all was the same as before, before E.A.

l

Things weren't the same, of course. I knew that, and Mother did, and M.N. certainly did. It was sort of funny that Father alone insisted on thinking they were. I began to wonder why he didn't get my nervous-stomach feeling once in a while, but I guess he never did.

So, even though things weren't exactly the same, they were O.K., right up to the time school began and E.A. and Stephen went to nursery school.

Then suddenly, everything changed, and kept on changing, and nothing has been the same since.

9

The first changes were nothing you could put your finger on, exactly. It was, as my Mother said, just "something in the air."

Mother drove Stephen and Edgar Allan to their first morning in nursery school. For them, too, it was the church school. I guess maybe because Sally Ann was there, and it made sense to have them all in the same place.

Father had thought a lot about nursery school for E.A. Since he was its principal, Father couldn't very well not send him to his own school. Besides, since he *was* in charge there, he could watch, and see exactly what happened when it happened, if anything happened.

But Father didn't tell the teacher of the pre-school classes (there were two: one in the morning and another in the afternoon) that the two kids coming in weren't really from the same family. I guess it was his way of testing the woman, to see how she felt about a Negro in school at all. She was a pretty girl, and Father hoped she wouldn't disappoint him.

It turned out she didn't. When Mother brought Stephen and Edgar Allan into class, the teacher didn't say anything and didn't, so Mother said, drop a stitch. She just said hello and let them move right in with the other kids.

And none of them objected either. After all, when the average age in a class is a little more than three, who knows enough to think of reasons to be unpleasant?

So the morning went along just fine.

The "something in the air" occurred afterwards.

And it was very simple. All the mothers of the kids in the class had driven to school at noon to pick up their children. My mother was among them. They all sat there, in their cars, waiting.

The kids came out, and each one naturally went to his own car, or, if someone was driving someone else home, to that car. Stephen and E.A. came out together and, seeing Mother and the station wagon, let out a holler and ran to meet her.

The other mothers, seeing E.A. for the first time even though they had heard about him before, watched very closely. They watched as he and Stephen, laughing together, climbed into the back seat, and as each leaned over the seat to kiss Mother on the cheek. Then Mother drove away.

The something in the air, Mother said, was the look that came from the parked cars. A little surprise, that E.A. really did exist, and then questioning. What is *he* doing *here* with our children?

Mother told Father all this after dinner, as they were having coffee. I had stuck around because I didn't feel like doing homework right away, and because I could tell Mother had something on her mind.

"You're imagining things, Eleanor," my father said. "And that's understandable. But I can't believe that those women would think a three-year-old is a threat to their own children."

"He's not just any three-year-old, Robert. He's black. *That's* the threat," my mother said. "I will give you five to one that by tomorrow afternoon you'll have three calls from three separate mothers, each wanting to know exactly what that child is doing in that school."

(My mother, though she looks sort of quiet and firm and likes to think a lot, is really a gambler at heart. Father says that when he proposed to her, she gave him three-to-one odds he couldn't support her the first year of their marriage. She won, too, and so she went to work to help out.)

And Mother was right this time, as well. The next afternoon, when she went to pick up E.A. and Stephen, there were the uneasy mothers sitting and watching again. And in a few cars, I guess because their wives had made them leave work and come to see for themselves, sat fathers, too. Both, Mother said, watched hawk-like as E.A. climbed into the back seat.

By four o'clock that day, Father had had not three but four calls, and had done his best to explain and to soothe people. This happened at the school, in his office, and I was sorry about that. Because when I heard all about this, that mean stomach thing grumbled again, and I wondered a little what Father *had* said to those people.

Nothing much happened then for a while, mostly because we had a weekend. But in church that Sunday, you could notice a change in the way people looked at Father and listened to him. It was as though they were trying to listen *in back* of his words, trying to figure out what he was *really* saying, and really thinking. And what he was going to do next.

This was silly. Father just went ahead and gave his usual sort of sermon. It was all about the last being first and the first being last into heaven, and how the first and the last would have to arrive hand-in-hand, working together, to gain admittance. If the words he said meant anything special, it was because of the way people were listening, not because of the way he was saying them.

I was glad that day that E.A. and Stephen weren't yet allowed to come to church with us. My mother says there's no point in having anyone under four try to sit still in a pew when what is going on won't mean anything to them anyway. S.A. herself had only just begun to join us, and she was difficult enough to keep still.

(One nice thing, though, was the way S.A. would look up at Father when he spoke. You could tell she thought he was the tallest and most important man in the world.)

Not so many people came by afterwards that day to say hello, but it was raining, which is rare for our town, and they probably were in a hurry to get home out of the bad weather.

One more thing I remember about that Sunday. I began to wonder if that awful feeling in the pit of my stomach was going to hang on for the rest of my life. And I looked up the word "ulcer" in the dictionary when I got home.

10

During the next weeks, things were a little more serious than just "something in the air." One afternoon,
Father got two calls from parents of children at the church
school saying their kids were changing to the public
schools. Father asked why, but I guess the people who
called never really said. They didn't have to.

My father, instead of getting angry, invited both
families over for tea the next afternoon, so they could
see how little they had to fear from Edgar Allan, and
how happy and normal he was. But they didn't come.

And a few days after that, someone in the hall of
my school went by me very fast and very sneaky and
whispered, "Nigger lover!"

I turned around to see who it was, but I couldn't tell.
I was angry and sort of scared, I admit. But scared only
because there were a hundred kids in the hall and any
one of them could have said it.

The funny thing, from the way things happened
so fast, you'd have thought that everyone in town had
kids, or brothers and sisters, in the church school. This
was ridiculous. They couldn't have. Our town isn't that
small, and we have maybe a dozen churches of different
kinds and lots of schools.

But by the way the word spread, I began to suspect
there were only one hundred families in the whole town.
I don't think I'll ever understand why E.A. was suddenly
so important. A lot of people had known he was around
during the summer. Maybe there was a difference in

his being a cute little kid during the summer, and being black when he got to school in the fall.

I was careful about what I did then during school time. When I walked through the halls between classes, I didn't carry too many books. The reason was I wanted one hand free to grab whoever it was who said what he said if he said it again.

I didn't have to wait very long. One morning, as I was going through the doors at the school's entrance, I heard it: "Nigger lover!" I grabbed out in that direction, and latched onto Tommy Ditford.

We stared at each other a minute. It was nervous, sort of, because I could see he was scared, but mad, too. I looked at him and then, almost whispering but at the same time firm-like, said, "Yes. He's my brother, Edgar Allan."

Tommy didn't say anything at all. I let go his arm and turned away, walking straight to my homeroom.

As I walked, a little faster than I do most times, I felt different somehow. Older, and stronger, though that was nutty. But I knew *why* I felt this way, changed a little. It was what Father always used to say, that you have to choose, you have to pick one way to live your life and then stick with it, all the way through.

So I guess I had chosen.

11

When I told my father what had happened to me with Tommy Ditford, he said he was proud of me. But what he really wondered was what, if anything, was being said to M.N. in her school. He even asked me if I knew.

I didn't, of course. M.N. wasn't talking to me any more than to anyone else. She went to school each day, very quietly, and came back the same way, never saying a word about E.A. or what was happening. She paid no more attention to him than before.

I was willing to bet that "Snooty" Flynn and "Fats" Browning, among others, had had a few things to say. And I can guess what M.N. answered. (I'm not this smart ordinarily. I just remember what happened that one afternoon before.)

For the next few days, things kept changing. Everything, that is, except "A Man for All Seasons," Thomas More.

I had come across him because of a movie someone made, and I read a really great play about how More stood up to Henry VIII and wouldn't approve publicly of what the King was doing, just to help him. It was scary, because what More really did was just keep his mouth shut, never saying a word to anyone one way or the other. And it was this silence that got him, and sent him to the Tower of London a prisoner.

I was glad I had read it.

Mother and Father, meanwhile, had a lot of their serious talks in the study, mostly at night when we were all upstairs. They had a record-breaker, though, one afternoon, when two men who belong to our church came by to talk to Father.

I don't think I have ever heard Mother and Father argue, but I suspect they came pretty close to it that afternoon. I don't know exactly what the men said to Father, but afterwards, after the serious talk between him and Mother, I had the feeling that things were really getting kind of tense.

My mother walked out of the study, and her face was set in a way I'd never seen before. She looked determined about something, and sort of angry and sad at the same time.

I looked into the study and found Father just sitting there, looking out the back window into our yard, and rocking. I stood there a minute or so, thinking he would sense I was there and turn around, but he didn't. So I waited another minute.

"Hello," I said.

Father swung around in his chair. "Hello, Michael," he said.

"Feel like walking a little?"

Father looked at me a minute, strangely, I thought, and then nodded. He got up, put his pipe in his pocket, and then turned again towards me. He was smiling.

"You're a good son to have," he told me.

I didn't say anything. There's not much you can say when someone says something nice about you. "Thanks" sounds sort of silly.

It was late afternoon, and the shadows from the eucalyptus and palm trees reached and passed us from the other side of the street as we walked. We didn't talk right away. Father had one hand in his pocket, and held his unlit pipe in the other. I was Prince Philip again, but without the throne-room.

After a while, I thought maybe if I started him off, Father would talk by himself later. So I started.

"What did those men want, who came this afternoon?" I asked.

Father turned to look at me a moment, sort of study-ing me. "You're a big fellow for your age," he said. "In your thinking, I mean."

That's another thing you can't say much to.

"What those men wanted," said Father, "was to know whether we're going to keep Edgar Allan or not."

"What else would we do with him?" I wanted to know.

"Well, Michael," Father said, "E.A. isn't really ours yet. Remember the testing period? Well, we're still in that. We have some time before a final decision is made, by us and by the adoption agency."

"That's silly," I said quickly. "They can see E.A. is happy with us. What would they want to take him away for?"

"They wouldn't, unless we wanted them to."

"You mean if we wanted to give him back, we could?"

"That's right," said Father. "If we wanted to, we could give E.A. back."

"Well, we don't want to. Do we?" My stomach hurt. For the first time, I was frightened for E.A.

"No," Father said. "We don't. But sometimes there are things we have to do that we don't really want to. Maybe giving E.A. back is one of those."

"What will the men from the church do if we give him back?"

"Nothing. It's what they'll do if we don't," he said.

Father didn't talk then, for a while. So I didn't. I just waited for him to begin again.

"What the men from the church said, Michael," he said after a very long time, "was that if we decided to keep Edgar Allan, the church might ask me to leave."

"Oh," I said. "What did you tell them?"

"Nothing."

"Nothing?"

"No. I listened. I let them tell me how they felt about E.A. and the church and the town we live in."

"Is that why Mother is mad?" I asked. "Because of the men?"

"No, Michael. Your mother is angry because I wouldn't say anything to them."

I thought about this a moment. "What did she want you to say?"

"That we were definitely going to keep Edgar Allan."

"But that would have meant you wouldn't be minister here any more," I said.

"Perhaps. Perhaps not. Your mother thinks not."

"What do *you* think?"

"I don't know yet. You know, Michael, sometimes what seems like a good idea, something that is good and honest and worthwhile, sometimes you run into a lot of trouble trying to hang onto it."

I waited, scared, with my hand on my belt.

"Sometimes," Father went on, "you have to make a choice between the idea and the real world that surrounds the idea. A choice, say, between one person and six, like our family."

And you know what I thought about then? Mary Nell. And I was thankful that Father had said what he said to me, instead of to her. When Mary Nell has the advantage, she never lets it go.

And right after that, after I had the idea about M.N., I had another idea. What about the "whole man" Father used to talk about?

A whole man, it seemed to me, would know exactly what to do if something like this happened. And what to say.

But Father didn't, and I couldn't understand why.

I had trouble getting to sleep that night.

12

As it turned out, the reason Father didn't say anything to the men from the church then was that he wanted to say something to them later, in his own way and in his own time. And his own time was the Sunday that came right afterwards.

It was a short sermon Father gave. It started out pretty much like his usual ones, except that about half-way through he began talking about how the Bible says a "little child shall lead them." What Father did, without really saying so, was make the little child Edgar Allan and *them* other Negroes.

It was nonsense, Father said, to imagine that one child could bring hundreds of others, whole families, into a new town or a new city. A child without family, who could barely speak, who simply wanted the opportunity to live as other children lived. That *some people* were afraid of a single child was a measure of how *some people* were afraid of everything the world offered.

Father said it was better by far, when walking into an unfamiliar dark room, to carry a flashlight. That way when something seemed to threaten you from a corner, all you had to do was turn the light in that direction and find out once and for all if the threat was a real one or only a shadow.

For his part, Father knew that one small child was perhaps as shadowy a fear as had been felt for a long time.

It was a good sermon. Father had told some people they were prejudiced (who didn't know that?) but he had told them without making them mad. It was tricky. I was proud of him, and Mother was, too. I looked around as Father spoke, and saw some people looking nervous and uncomfortable, and one or two who had sort of funny smirks on their faces. But most people just listened quietly. You couldn't tell what they were thinking.

Afterwards, not too many of them came up to speak to Father at the door of the church, but it didn't matter. That night I slept like a rock.

13

But waking up the next morning wasn't much fun.

I could sense something was funny the minute I stood up. Everything was quiet inside the house, but outside you could hear a sort of scraping sound.

I went to my window and looked down into the front yard. There was Father, raking a burned place in the grass. And Mother was down near the street, picking some kind of paper out of the bushes.

I got dressed very fast, sloshed a handful of water on my face, beat my hair into place, and ran downstairs.

I walked down the path to where Father was finishing with the rake. He looked up from his work, but didn't say anything. I stood there and looked at the charred place.

It was a funny sort of burn. I looked one way at it, and then another, and suddenly I realized that no matter which way you looked at it, it was the same thing: a cross.

There were a few bigger ashes raked to one side of the burn. They must have been part of the cross before it fell over onto the ground, and burned the grass. There was a shallow hole at one end of the gray spot.

I looked at Father, and he still wouldn't say anything.

"I thought people only did this in the South," I said.

My father thought a minute, and then sort of grinned. "Well, Michael," he said, "we *are* south of San Francisco."

I didn't think this was so funny, but I decided not to say so. "Who did it?" I asked instead.

"We don't know, Michael," Father answered, and he stopped smiling. "I haven't the faintest idea. It could have been lots of people, I suppose."

Father bent down to pick up the pieces of burned wood, and we turned to walk back into the house.

A movement from one of the windows upstairs caught my eye, and I looked up.

It was Mary Nell, ducking back behind the curtains, but not fast enough to be hidden completely. For some reason, I never thought of telling Father she had been watching. Perhaps it was because I suddenly noticed how tired he looked, as though he had been up most of the night.

At breakfast, everything seemed pretty much the same. On the outside. But if you looked hard, you could see Mother's hands shaking as she served the table; you could see she looked nearly as worn out as Father. Neither wanted to talk about the cross, or what the papers had been. They tried to pretend everything was O.K. as usual.

Of course, none of this touched E.A. himself. Or S.A. or Stephen. I guess they were too young, for one thing. And their playmates were too young, too, to be like Tommy Ditford or Snooty or Fats.

Maybe Sally Ann was aware of the "something in the air," but she wasn't saying anything. I guess there wasn't much she could have said. She's a great teacher, but to take on a whole town is a lot for a five-year-old, going on six.

14

As I thought about the cross that day on my way to school, I was almost sorry that what had happened hadn't happened the week before. Father could have used it for his sermon, and that would really have shaken some people. As it *did* happen, it was in the middle of a long string of things that came along, and so it got sort of lost, when it shouldn't have been allowed to be.

I nearly got into a fight over Edgar Allan that morning at school. It was Tommy Ditford again, but this time there were a few other guys who said the same kinds of things he did.

It wasn't that I got smart and realized I couldn't take five kids on at one time. What it was that kept us apart was the bell that ended recess. But it was a close thing, and all I could think of for those few minutes were the martyrs of long ago who died for whatever they believed.

Not that that's what I was planning. I like living a lot. But it was just one of those things that floats into your mind and hangs around for a while. Like a commercial.

When I got home, Mother was just turning into the driveway from shopping. She got out of the car, left her bundles on the seat, and started towards the house, calling to me, "Michael, bring those things into the kitchen, will you, please?"

So I did, and I missed the first part of the serious talk she and Father had already begun.

What it was about was an incident at the grocery store. I guess the checkout lady had kept Mother waiting a very long time, and then, when Mother's turn finally came, she closed the line. So, Mother had to go to another clerk, and then to another. Finally, I guess, Mother got mad and said something about it. But no one answered her, and no one served her.

After a while, Mother just left all her groceries in the cart where it was standing, and walked out of the store.

I imagine, though I don't really know, that the checkout lady probably thought this was just fine as far as she was concerned. She's a dragon, anyway, and hates almost everybody.

It was nearly dark when M.N. arrived home for dinner. Right away you could see, by looking at her just once, that she had something on her mind, too.

Dinner was good, and fast, and then Sally Ann and Stephen and E.A. were all put to bed. When Mother came downstairs, M.N. and Father and I were waiting for her in the study.

It was the first time I had ever been actually invited to a serious talk. Father had asked me. M.N. had something she wanted to say to him and to Mother, and I guess he felt I was old enough, and the problem was important enough, for me to be included. I didn't like it very much.

That was mostly because, as I said before, when M.N. has the advantage, she never loses it. That night, it took her maybe fourteen seconds to get it, and keep it.

15

"I know who put up the cross last night," M.N. began. "I know, and I'm not going to tell you who did it."

"Probably some of Snooty's friends, or yours," I said.

"It wasn't, either," M.N. said to me. "They were older." She blushed, remembering she wasn't going to tell who did it. I figured it was some of the older guys in her school.

"What good would it do to know exactly who?" Mother asked. "We got their message."

"Well," M.N. said, sort of loud like she was being scolded for something, "I'm not going to say anything more, except that I know. And I agree with them!"

I knew what Mother's face would look like, so I glanced at Father's. I couldn't tell anything. Maybe he hadn't heard. Or maybe I looked too late. He just looked up at M.N. and waited.

"You can't mean that, M.N.," Mother said quietly. "Not really."

"I do mean it, I do! Really!" Mary Nell answered fast. "We're just not the only people who live here, you know. Who are we to do what no one else wants to?"

"Just Christians, Mary Nell," Father said.

"That doesn't make any sense at all. Is what will happen to us, and to Edgar Allan, Christian?"

"What do you mean?" asked my father.

"Just this," said M.N. "I mean that there are rules here, rules which everybody follows because they want to. People have the right to live the way they want, and only with the kind of people around they like."

"So do we," said Mother, "since we're people, too. And we happen to like living with Edgar Allan around."

"*I* don't!" M.N. almost shouted. "I don't at all!"

"Why? How does his being here do you any harm?" Father wanted to know.

"Ohhh!" Mary Nell said shrugging. "You'll just never understand! But *I* can see what's going to happen even if you can't. If E.A. stays, there will be lots more trouble, just like what's been happening. Michael will get into fights and Mother will be pushed off a sidewalk or something worse. And you'll wind up with no one at all coming to church on Sundays. If the church even lets you stay."

"What will happen to you, M.N.?" asked Mother. "What do you see for yourself?"

M.N. looked at Mother a minute, and then at Father for almost as long before saying anything. "What I can see," she said, "is that my entire life will be ruined, is all, and yours, too. And not only won't I ever speak to either of you again, if he stays, but I'll *never* speak to him, either. I'll just leave altogether, and live somewhere else."

"That's childish, dear, running away," Mother said.

"Call it what you want to. Elizabeth Flynn agrees with me, and so does her mother. I can live with them until I'm through high school. They promised me I could."

"That *would* ruin your life for sure," Mother said with a funny smile.

"You can laugh all you want!" M.N. shouted. "But I'm dead serious. I'll leave, and that's that. I promise I will, you'll see! I refuse to let you ruin everything for me!"

"E.A. doesn't hurt my life much," I snuck in, fast and low.

"Ohhh! *Your* life can't ever be hurt, because you just don't let anyone else in it. Except your dumb English kings and barons and all. Of course it doesn't hurt you, you dummy!"

I decided not to answer Mary Nell, at least not right then. But I was mad, and I could feel myself get red, which made me madder.

It was quiet then for a minute or so. I looked over at Father.

He was just sitting in his chair, looking at M.N. every once in a while. His hands rested on the arms of his rocking chair, palms up, as though he was balancing something I couldn't see. If he was weighing M.N. against E.A., he had an easy choice, *I* thought. I'd take Edgar Allan any time.

"Mary Nell," Father said, after thinking a little. "What you may not understand is that E.A. isn't here for your mother and me, or for you children. He's here because we think it is good for him to be here. Because he can learn more and better with us than he could alone, or in an orphanage somewhere. Because he can have a better start in life this way."

"That's just swell, for now," M.N. said. "But when he gets older, what happens then? He won't be white, and he can't help being black. What sort of life will he have then?"

"Edgar Allan will never doubt who or what he is," said Mother, sort of strong now.

"That's because the town won't let him, is all," M.N. said.

"It's because as he grows up," Mother argued, "he will learn about himself and his country and his background."

"As a slave?" M.N. asked sharply.

"That's unworthy of you, Mary Nell," Father said.

"I don't care," she answered. "I don't care at all. I'm just warning you what will happen if he stays, and telling you how I feel about it. It seems to me that it ought to make some difference to you. After all, I am your *real* daughter, not just someone you pitied and took in for silly-sounding reasons. You *have* to pay attention, I would think. There's me, and Michael, and S.A. and Stephen, and Mother, to think of."

"Don't worry about me, dear," said Mother. "I can stand up by myself."

"So can I!" M.N. cried. "But that doesn't change anything! If you keep Edgar Allan here, and the town is against it, you're sacrificing six lives for one. And that isn't fair to the rest of us. That one isn't even really yours!"

16

It was a pretty short serious talk that night. Mary Nell was so worked up about the whole thing she just couldn't talk any more, so she went up to her room.

There wasn't much for me to do, either, or to say. I figured whatever had to be said Father could say to M.N., or to Mother, or to any one else. So I got up and went for a walk, by myself.

There were a lot of things to think about. There were two M.N. things, I figured. For one, you had to admire her in a way. She knew her feelings were wrong, but what she felt she felt, and that was that. At least, she wasn't pretending anything, which is pretty honest.

For the other, it suddenly hit me that maybe Mary Nell wanted to be a friend of mine.

After I got over being mad at her about "my" kings and barons, it came to me that maybe she thought my special world was O.K. after all, and might even be interesting if she could get into it. M.N. wasn't mad at me for saying what I said about my life not being ruined by Edgar Allan. She was mad because she knew it was true, because I sort of have things organized in my head.

So I decided I would try to be a little kinder to M.N. than before, and see if she really did want to be friends. It wouldn't be very easy, because she still wasn't always very nice. But I could try a little, anyway.

Then I thought about God. What I thought wasn't much, except that our serious talk seemed to be one of those places where He wasn't. In fact, as I thought about it, He hadn't been around much anywhere in our town just then.

That must mean something, I thought, if what Mother says is right. So I promised myself to be on the lookout more for Him, in both places, at home and in the town, too.

And then my old ugly feeling came back. It hit when I realized that a lot of the good things Mother had said to M.N., Father should have said. And I couldn't help worrying just a little about E.A. Nothing really serious, though. My stomach just wouldn't take serious worrying.

So I pushed the worry-thoughts away, and decided, on that walk, that someday I would write this book. It would be a way of explaining to Edgar Allan (when he could read, naturally) what happened in our family, and in our town. So he would know, I guess, that his main problem wasn't what he was, but what he looked like. No one seemed to care that he was happy and smart and cute. All that mattered was he was black.

I figured out how I would start my book, too, but then, of course, I forgot about it until now. I *was* going to start by "talking" to him, trying to explain simply what prejudice was.

It was supposed to be something like this.

"Michael," Edgar Allan would say, "do you know what prejudice is?"

"Yes, E.A. I do."

"What?" he would ask me then.

"It's when no one likes you," I answer.

"But why, why doesn't anybody like you?" E.A. says.

"Because," I answer. "Just because."

17

When I came home from school the next afternoon, Edgar Allan was gone.

And everything seemed sort of unreal.

What had happened was that our lives, in one afternoon, had all been put back the way they were a few months before. It should have been easy to slide into being a family of just six again, but it wasn't.

On the inside, what had happened was that we had all been hurt in a funny kind of way. I think everyone, except maybe S.A. and Stephen, felt shorter that night than when we started out in the morning.

Dinner was sad and sort of funny, too. M.N. hadn't known E.A. had been sent back until just that minute, when she sat down at the table. She had been late coming home from school, and I guess she hadn't noticed anything different yet.

It was Mother who answered M.N.'s question. She told M.N. what, I figured, she had told Sally Ann and Stephen that afternoon, and what I guess she felt she had to say again, since they were both at the table and listening. But M.N. knew the truth.

"They found Edgar Allan's real family, M.N.," Mother answered.

"They *what?*"

"The agency telephoned us this afternoon, while Stephen and Sally Ann were napping. They told us E.A.'s family had been found, and wanted very much to have him back again."

"You're kidding!" M.N. gasped. "That's ridiculous!"

"Why is it?" Sally Ann wanted to know reasonably. "If children can be lost, why can't a mother and father get lost sometimes, too?"

"That's right, dear," Mother said to S.A. And then she went on, but speaking down sort of, into her plate, not looking at M.N. or me, or at Father. "Your father and I, knowing how anxious E.A.'s parents would be to see him again, got him dressed and packed a little suitcase."

"That was when Stephen and I were asleep," S.A. added. "Or we would have helped."

"Then, M.N.," Mother said, "your father drove Edgar Allan away."

There was a moment which I couldn't describe to anyone who wasn't right there. What I wanted to do most then was get up from the table and run out into the street and race like crazy around block after block, just to get everything out of my mind.

What I didn't want most to do was look at my father.

I looked at Mother instead. For someone who thought a lot, I guess she had stopped thinking about E.A. and started loving him as one of her own the minute he arrived. She wouldn't look at any of us, but you could see underneath, sort of, to where she was mad. More than mad and more than angry, I guess. Mostly at Father, for if she understood why he had done as he had, you could see she didn't agree with it. And you could see she was blaming herself as well, for somehow letting him do what he did.

"That's not all, Mommy," Sally Ann said, breaking a kind of spell. "Tell M.N. the rest. Tell her what they said."

"What *who* said, dear?" Mother asked.

"*His* mother and father, E.A.'s," Sally Ann told her.

"Oh, you're right," Mother pretended to remember. "They asked that we thank Sally Ann and S.P. for taking such good care of Edgar Allan, and for teaching him so many useful things. Most especially, thank you to Sally Ann."

"We were taking care of E.A., don't you see, M.N.?" Sally Ann offered. "We were just baby-sitting," and she giggled a little. So did Stephen Paul.

M.N. just sat there, dead still, her mouth sort of open.

There wasn't anything else to do, really. You couldn't start talking about something else then, because Edgar Allan was on everyone's mind.

What exactly each person was thinking you couldn't know. I suspect Mother, and maybe M.N., were thinking what I was: what being taken back must have meant to E.A. And what it would mean as he grew older, no matter where he was, or with what family.

What, I wondered, had E.A. himself been told? You couldn't have told him his parents had been found. When he got back he would know right away it wasn't true. And then I realized why—or, at least, I thought I knew why—E.A. had left so suddenly.

Father was tearing the band-aid off as fast as he could. He was trying to erase a page in our lives, to write over the past few months. He probably thought that giving E.A. a chance to say goodby to S.A. and Stephen would only bring questions to all of their minds, and make leaving even more difficult for E.A. And it would have made it worse for himself, for Father.

Because I knew one thing definitely now. Father would never have been able to tell E.A. the truth, ever. He would never have had the courage to tell him that a town had beaten down his family and made them afraid, made them forget him and remember only themselves.

18

Dinner ended then. It was rather short.

My mother got up without saying a word to anyone, took a sweater from the front closet, and went outside. A few seconds later, I heard the car start up. She was gone for more than an hour.

M.N. stood up next, and began clearing the table. She didn't look at anyone, and she didn't ask for any help. She just ducked her head and went to work.

Father left the table and went into the living-room. He turned on the television set, sort of loud. Sally Ann and Stephen followed him, and sat in front of the screen, watching some program or other. Then Father went into his study and sat in his rocker, just rocking and looking out into the backyard.

Finally I got up, too, and took my plate and glass into the kitchen, because I hadn't anything else to do right then anyway. I thought about trying to talk to M.N., because I remembered the promise I had made to myself the night before.

I figured she felt guilty and mad at everybody. Still, we *are* only a couple of years apart, so I thought maybe this was as good a time as any to start being friends. What happened was that what I meant to say, when I was thinking about it, came out entirely different.

"Still want to move in with Elizabeth Flynn?" something made me ask.

"Ohhh, why don't you just get out of here? Go bother Father!" M.N. spun around and looked mean. "Father's the one who did this, not me!"

"Why tell me? I was here, too, you nit!"

"But you're so stupid, you miss everything except historical things! Ohhhh," M.N. shouted, "I hate this whole family! This whole town!"

"That's nutty," I said. "You're just like everyone else in the whole town, anyway. Everyone feels just the way you said they would. Just the way you said *you* did!"

"Well, it's not my fault! Can I help it?"

"Who else would? Father's not able to help *anybody*."

"Damn it!" M.N. screamed, and threw a dish-towel against the wall. "Damn it, damn it!"

It was pretty quiet there, for a minute.

"What did you want him to do?" I asked after a while.

M.N. calmed down a little. She looked at me sort of differently, with interest, I guess. "Did you think he would ever give E.A. back?" she asked.

"Not really," I said. "If I did, it was just a tiny thought, not a real one. It's not being the kind of person I thought he was."

"Me, neither," M.N. said. "I don't see why. I just don't see why."

"You," I told her.

"Oh, Michael," M.N. sighed. "That would only be part of the reason."

I thought a moment. "I guess you're right," I said. "Did you think they would stand up to you, Mother and him?"

"I don't know."

"Did you want them to?" I asked.

M.N. thought for a very long time. "Yes," she said finally, all quiet now. "I guess I did, really."

"You certainly have a funny way of going about getting the things you want," I said.

M.N. changed right back into the old, nasty M.N. She swung her fist at me, and I ducked as she said, "Ohhh, get out of here, you idiotic little . . . little *for*eigner!"

So I did. I walked out of the kitchen and into the living-room. I looked into the study as I passed and saw Father sitting there, rocking.

I could have asked him if he wanted to go for a walk. I thought of it.

But I didn't do it.

19

Life was quiet then for a while. Everyone went his own way, except, of course, for S.A. and Stephen, who just went on pretty much as before. Sally Ann missed E.A. There was no doubt of that. But it wasn't a sad kind of missing. It was more like she had lost her favorite toy. She just hadn't quite so much to do, or so many people to teach.

She wondered where E.A.'s family lived, and whether it was far away. And what E.A. would do now about school if they lived in another city. Once she came to ask if I thought we would be able to visit Edgar Allan sometime. I can't remember what I said to her. Whatever it was, it was short.

Mother was the quietest of all. She did the things she had to, and remembered to go to the store, and pick up the two little kids at school, and to cook dinner. But you didn't hear her use one extra word more than she had to; she said "yes" and "no" and "ask your father" and everyone knew that it would take time for her to be herself again.

Father kept to his church and to the study there, which was just as well, as far as I could see. When he came home, he spent his time playing with S.A. and Stephen. It was sort of nice watching, if you *happened* to be watching, but you never forgot that he was just playing, pretending, that is, and that he was really thinking about something else.

Also, it meant he didn't have to talk with Mother. For Mother hadn't spoken very much to Father since

E.A. left, and they both tried hard not to be alone to-gether. They hadn't argued, really. But they had. It was one of those things I can't explain. It was more like they were both afraid of each other, and of suddenly saying something they would regret later.

M.N. spent most of her time in her room. I never know what she does there, but whatever it is, she does it quietly. I used to pass her door, once in a while, and stand outside a minute—not really eavesdropping; she does that, not me—but trying to get a clue. There weren't any.

I did a lot of reading in those days. I read about Charles I who lost his head, and about Mary of Scotland, and even a little about Bernadotte of Sweden, who really didn't belong with the rest of my people at all. Still, *he* had guts. He stood up to Napoleon and got to be his own king, sort of. He was what you would have to call a "whole man."

Then, one day after school, M.N. and I were sitting outside on the grass together. We weren't talking. Just sitting. It was sort of funny, because we had never done this before. It just happened, like we both felt very tired at the same time and sat down to rest together.

We were sitting there, looking up at the trees, when S.A. and Stephen Paul came out from the house. So there were four of us, just sitting, one afternoon.

From almost nowhere, a man began walking up the path. I hadn't heard a car door slam, or seen him coming. He just appeared, an O.K.-looking guy with no hat, no briefcase, or anything like that.

He got to where we all were, smiled and sat down at the same time, just as if he belonged there. Sally Ann didn't think he did and so right away she asked him who he was.

"My name is Joe Ryder," he said, and smiled at her. "I work for a newspaper in San Francisco."

"What are you doing here?" M.N. asked very very fast when she heard this. She was really sort of mean-sounding.

"Just sitting here, wondering what you're all thinking about."

"Nothing that would interest you, I'm sure," said
M.N.

"What was it you *thought* we were thinking about?"
I asked.

"Oh," Joe Ryder said, "I thought maybe you might
be thinking about Edgar Allan. Nothing very deep or
serious. Just maybe remembering him."

"Do *you* know E.A.?" Sally Ann asked happily. "We
took care of him."

"How did you do that?" asked Ryder.

"Well," said S.A., all smiles and full of pride, "we
were taking care of him until his own real family could
be found. And I taught him all kinds of things he would
need to know, when he grew up."

"That was nice of you. Was he a good student?" Ryder
asked.

"He was O.K.," S.A. decided after a minute. "He's
smarter than Stephen Paul here, but not quite so sm—"

"He was not smarter than me!" Stephen shot in.

"Well, in *some* things," S.A. said quickly. "Not in
everything. But in some things."

"Was he doing well in school?"

"That's silly," Sally Ann told Ryder. "You don't get
marks or grades in pre-school. You just learn simple
things there."

"I forgot," Joe Ryder said.

"Mr. Ryder," M.N. said, "why are you here, really?
What is it you want?"

He thought first. "I guess I came," he said finally,
"to find out about how you all felt towards Edgar Allan,
and about how he lived here. It would interest some
people who read our newspaper."

"I can't think how," M.N. said coldly. I was sort of
surprised. Knowing M.N. as I do, I would have thought
she would die to get her name in the paper. "Edgar Allan
lived with us, and he grew up a little, and then he went

• 70 •

away. That's all there is to it, if you must know. Nothing else."

"Just one of the family then, eh, Mary Nell?" he asked.

M.N. was startled for a second, because Ryder knew her name. But she came back strong.

"Just exactly, *Mis*ter Ryder. Just exactly that way," she told him.

"How did you feel about giving him away, then?" Ryder asked suddenly.

M.N. nearly jumped out of her skin. *His* voice was nearly as cold as hers had been, and I think she was frightened. And then she thought about S.A. and S.P. who were, of course, taking all this in.

"I don't know what you mean," she said, again sort of cool.

"We didn't do anything special," S.A. said. "We were just keeping him till his own mother and father could take care of him. He could have stayed as long as he wanted to."

"Sally Ann," said Ryder, smiling as nicely as he could at her. "Edgar Allan could have stayed as long as *you* all wanted, not as long as *he* wanted."

I stood up as fast as I could. "Mr. Ryder, it's our dinnertime," I said. "Maybe you better talk to my mother, or my father, if there's anything you want to know. All we know is what we've already told you."

M.N. was standing up, too. "I don't think," she said, "that you should ask Sally Ann any questions. Or Stephen, either. Or Michael or me, Mr. Ryder. Why don't you go away?"

"Why is everyone mad all of a sudden?" asked Sally Ann.

"Never mind," I told her. "Come on, let's go in."

"No," S.A. answered. "What did he mean, we could keep E.A.?"

"Nothing," I said. "He doesn't know anything. Come on, S.A."

"He must know *something*," she said. "He works for the newspaper."

I felt sort of sorry then for Joe Ryder, but only for a second. *He* couldn't know why M.N. and I were so quick so sudden. Still, he should have let it go, and he wouldn't.

But I didn't know that until the next day.

20

What happened was that Joe Ryder was a pretty smart guy. I guess when you're a reporter you have to be, to keep finding things out ahead of other people. Still, even though we found out how smart he was, I felt he was cheating, too.

What he did was wait until the next day. Stephen and Sally Ann, who is still only in kindergarten no matter what she *sounds* like, come home every day at lunch time since they have only a half-day of school.

For the last few weeks, Mother had been letting S.A. take charge of Stephen and E.A., and she would lead them home, which wasn't too far, whenever the weather was nice. It was nice the day Joe Ryder met S.A. and Stephen Paul and walked with them.

For some reason, Ryder explained what had really happened. I guess he felt he had to to get S.A. to tell him what had happened from her side of the story. He said that E.A. could have stayed, but that we sent him back ourselves. That he didn't have any real parents; they had died when he was a very small baby, which is how we got him, through the adoption agency. And that for some reason we had decided to send him back, to return him, because we were unhappy with him.

What Ryder wanted to know was why we were unhappy with Edgar Allan. What had happened that would make us send him away?

Naturally, S.A. and Stephen Paul didn't know what he was talking about. But they did know enough to be frightened and confused. Maybe that isn't what Ryder was trying to do, but that's sure what he did. Sally Ann came home crying like crazy, wanting Father to explain.

But Father wasn't home, so Mother tried. I guess she didn't do a good enough job for S.A. because when I came home, both S.A. and S.P. were outside waiting for me.

"Michael!" S.A. shouted when she saw me. "Michael!" and she ran down the path, Stephen Paul right behind her, and grabbed me around the waist, crying. Stephen snuck in close, too, and hung on as tight as he could.

"Michael," Sally Ann said at last through her sniffles, "why *did* we give E.A. away? We loved him, didn't we? *Why* did we? *Why?*

I tried to pull them both off me a little, so we could move over under a big tree. "Now listen," I said, "what happened wasn't your fault, S.A. Or yours, either, Stephen. In any way at all."

"Whose is it?" Stephen asked.

"Whose fault is it, Michael?" Sally Ann asked, too. "We loved him. *I* did. *I* loved him."

"Me, too," said Stephen.

"So *we* wouldn't have wanted him to go—ever!" S.A. cried.

"Well, now," I said, sort of stalling because I didn't really know what to say next. "What did Mother tell you?"

"I don't know," Sally Ann said blankly.

"What do you mean, you don't know? What did she say?"

"Well," Sally Ann hesitated, "I couldn't understand. She said it wasn't our fault."

"There, you see," I said quickly. "That's exactly what *I* said."

"She said," Sally Ann said, her eyes beginning to fill with tears again, "that it wasn't anyone's fault. That it was something that just didn't work out."

"Well," I said, "that's simple, then, isn't it?"

"But what does it *mean?*" Sally Ann asked.

"Well, it means that it hasn't anything to do with us, that's what," I tried.

"But it has!" S.A. shouted. "*Mr. Ryder* told us so! He said E.A. could have stayed forever if we had wanted him to. *I* wanted him to!"

"Me, too," Stephen added.

"Me, too," I said finally.

Sally Ann had stopped crying, and just stood where she was a moment. At last she took Stephen by the hand and started to walk back towards the house.

I watched her go, determined sort of, wanting someone to explain once and for all to her. She stopped suddenly, and pulled Stephen Paul to her as she turned back to face me.

"Michael?"

"What?"

"Who decides when things work out?"

I didn't know what to say.

"If Daddy could give Edgar Allan away, why couldn't he give us away? S.P. or me?"

21

I don't think I could have answered S.A.'s questions in an hour, even if I'd tried. But she didn't give me that much time. She just asked her questions and then knowing, I guess, that she was asking the wrong person, pulled Stephen Paul back into the house, where they stayed until dinner, quiet in S.A.'s room.

A little later, M.N. came home and came up to my room. She knocked on the door, which was a first.

"Michael?"

"What is it?"

"May I come in?"

"O.K.," I said. I decided not to put my book down yet. You never knew about M.N.

"Oh, Michael," M.N. sighed, sinking down right away onto the rug. "What *are* we going to do now?"

I put down my book. "About what?"

"About everything. Just everything."

"What does Snooty Flynn have to say about it?" I asked.

"Oh, don't be such a dummy," M.N. said. "I don't care about her, *or* about your old Fats Browning."

This was news. "Who then?" I asked.

"Us. You and me, and Father. Poor Father! I've tried to talk to him, but he just can't explain. I don't think even *he* knows why it all happened."

"Look," I said quickly, "if you want to worry about someone, it seems to me it's better to worry about S.A. and Stephen, or Mother."

"Well, what *are* we going to do, then?" M.N. asked again.

"Just wait and see what happens, I guess."

"But that's not nearly enough. We have to do something *more!*"

"I don't know what it would be," I said. And I didn't.

So we just sat there, M.N. on the rug and me on my bed. It was sort of nice, really, just to do that together.

22

At dinner that night, neither Sally Ann nor Stephen said anything at all about what had happened during the day. They didn't mention Joe Ryder, or what Mother had told them, or their fear. They just sat at the table and ate.

Sally Ann has never been able to keep from explaining, over and over again, whom she taught and what each day, even if it turns out to have been only Stephen. But that night she just sat quietly, and ate what was put in front of her.

She wouldn't look at me, or at M.N. or Mother. Neither would Stephen. I figured they had made their own decision of some kind, and had either decided to accept what Mother told them, or what Joe Ryder had.

What worried me a little was that if they chose what Joe Ryder said as the truth, what would they do?

But they didn't seem to be doing anything. Sally Ann helped Mother clear the dishes afterwards, and Stephen went straight up to his room to get ready for bed.

A little while later, S.A. followed him up. And then they both came down in their pajamas, kissed Mother and then Father good-night, and went back upstairs.

That was all there was to it. Almost.

About an hour later, they made a reappearance.

Father was in his study. Mother sat in front of the television set with M.N. and me, knitting and watching the news. It was she who noticed two skinny shadows creeping down the front stairs.

Mother turned around in her chair and saw Stephen and Sally Ann, each with a small suitcase, slipping down the last few steps and running for the front door. As the door opened, she stood up and called, "Robert!"

My father came out of his study. Mother pointed towards the front door, and moved in that direction. Father followed her.

M.N. and I rushed to the window. What we saw was S.A. and Stephen, hand in hand, walking quickly down the path towards the street. They had their suitcases in opposite hands, and walked very fast without looking back.

Father went to the door. "Sally Ann!" he called.

S.A. stopped, but didn't look back. When Father didn't call again right away, she and Stephen went on, turning right and starting up the street.

"Sally Ann!" Father called again.

And S.A. stopped again. Stephen Paul turned around. Finally, after a very long minute, S.A. turned, too, to see Father come out the front door and start down the path.

Then, as we watched, Father stopped, and held open his arms.

No one moved. I think my mother had stopped breathing. M.N. grabbed my hand and squeezed it, hard.

Stephen, without a word to Sally Ann, took his hand away from hers, and ran back towards Father, crying as loud as I've ever heard him. He came running up and jumped into Father's arms, which came around him so fast you could hardly see them move.

Sally Ann just watched. Then, after a moment, she turned around and started walking away from the house again.

I guess she had decided to go it alone.

"Sally Ann!" Father called again, just loudly enough for her to hear. She stopped and stood still, without turning.

Father, still holding Stephen Paul, walked down the path to her. When he reached her, Father took S.A.'s hand and turned her around. Together—Stephen being carried, and Sally Ann being towed—they came home.

23

The problem was, how to tell S.A. and Stephen what
had happened, without really telling them what had happened. I mean, Father couldn't just say that E.A. was black,
and belonged with other black people. It wasn't that easy,
for one thing. And it really wasn't true, for another.
For though it might have been true in our family's case,
it needn't have been.

Nor could Father tell Sally Ann and Stephen they
would never, ever be "given away" because they were
really *his*, and E.A. wasn't. S.A. would just remind him
what he used to say: "Everyone belongs in a way to everyone else, and has to have some responsibility for them."

I don't know what Father did say. He took Stephen
Paul upstairs, along with S.A. whom he still had by the
hand, and went with them into Stephen's room, and
closed the door.

What I *could* hear from downstairs—Mother and
M.N. were listening, too—was just a warm sound, the
comforting voice that hummed a little from upstairs,
a home kind of thing. Stephen stopped crying, and S.A.
listened all the way through.

It occurred to me, then, that while he wasn't so hot
with grown-up problems, Father was pretty good with
kids. And then I decided that I was only making an excuse
for his failing where it counted most.

Even with S.A. I guess maybe she decided that afternoon that if Father could give E.A. away, she and Stephen
would have to be extra good one hundred per cent of

the time, or be given away, too. That it must have been Father who decided when things worked out and when they didn't. Rather than wait for his decision, Sally Ann had decided she and Stephen might as well leave right away.

What Father had to do was convince her and Stephen that he loved them and that their fears were silly. He had had more than five years of proving this already to S.A., and more than three with Stephen. His job wasn't as big as all that.

The weeks that followed were more O.K. than before.

I have never really talked with Mother the way Father and I used to. I guess I always felt that since she was a mother and all, she would always be too busy with someone or something to take time out for just a walk. And it was hard getting her to sit down and relax and talk. She was always doing something else with her hands at the same time. So, what you had to do with Mother was sort of learn about her from watching, and sometimes from listening.

But, like what Mother says about God, you had to listen to more than just the things she said. You had to listen to the things she *didn't* say, too.

And what she didn't say after we sent E.A. away was a lot. I knew she was disappointed in every one of us. Mostly in Father, but also in M.N. and me.

I think with M.N. Mother could understand. With me, maybe she felt I should have spoken up and said something. But, thinking back, it would have been hard to do since I never really thought we would ever give Edgar Allan up.

I don't know what it was that made *her* give E.A. back. I am almost sure she didn't want to. That she and Father must have had their first really serious argument about it. But Father must have said something that made sense to her. Maybe it was about his job and supporting us, or about M.N. and what she would do. Maybe it was only about himself.

But I knew Mother had been as strong as she could be for as long as she could be. Maybe she gave up when she found out that she was standing all alone, that what had been planned and agreed on was falling apart and that she couldn't hold it all together single-handedly.

Stephen Paul came back to his normal self again. I guess maybe he had been so scared because Sally Ann was, and he mostly takes his orders from her. Which is really sort of good, because she's a good teacher, and an O.K. girl for almost six.

She didn't come back to normal quite so fast. I think S.A. had put Father on a kind of test, and was just watching and waiting for the first sign that meant she was in trouble again and might be sent away. It was silly, I thought, but I was also a lot older than she was.

Father knew S.A. was examining him, and testing all the time. He did everything he could to calm her down and show her she had nothing to fear. He even took her for two of *our* old walks. And when they came back after the second one, they were holding hands and S.A. was rattling on at a great rate the way she always had before. You could tell everything was going to be all right again between them soon.

M.N. and I spent a lot more time together. For some reason, I guess M.N. had decided I was more interesting than Fats or Snooty. I suspected that M.N. had run into the same kind of thing at her school as I did at mine.

I mean, except for us, no one in town had wanted E.A. around. But when he was gone, everyone sort of blamed us for it. Snooty and Fats might have thought E.A. was cute, but they wouldn't have missed him any more than any one else in town would have. But by the way M.N. was acting, I would have bet that they had blamed *her* for sending him away. Which was just something else silly to think and say. All it did was confuse people, and make you uncertain about who your friends were, and why.

One thing you could *almost* be sure of was your own family. It was nice, I guess, about M.N. and me. I let her read some of my books, and I showed her the drawings I had made of each English king since Henry VII. We even got more interested in Bernadotte than in my usual British crowd. Mostly he appealed to M.N. because he married a beautiful woman who stood by him through thick and thin and got to be Princess and then Queen of Sweden. This hooked old M.N. like crazy.

Actually, M.N. was turning out O.K. after all. I'm not sure if we still had E.A. she would have felt differently, but I know she would have behaved better.

It's hard to want to be one thing (one of the girls) and have to be another (a minister's daughter). M.N. was just learning I guess that maybe the two could be mixed together to make one good thing. You just had to make up your mind to be yourself. Or, both yourselves at the same time, which adds up to one yourself.

It turned out that Joe Ryder, after talking to a lot of people, had gone back to San Francisco and written an article about us in the newspaper. I found out about it at school one day. Someone showed it to me, and I brought it back to M.N.

It was just one long piece, and it didn't say anything bad about *us*, which was a surprise. What it said, though, was about our town. He didn't mention any names, but he made you think about our town in a funny way. Not funny so much, because what he wrote was very serious. But he made you blame *everybody* for what had happened to E.A.

That was the one thing he said he cared about: what about E.A. himself? What had being given back done to him? It was the one thing I hadn't wanted to think about, and the one that Joe Ryder wanted everyone to.

He had talked to E.A.'s teacher at pre-school, and to the parents of some of the other little kids who were in his class. The parents all tried to sound sort of sensible and grown-up, but they came out sounding mean and sneaky. I guess this is what Joe Ryder wanted them to sound like.

From the way S.A. felt when she thought Father would give *her* away, you could just begin to figure out the way E.A. himself felt about being given away.

"But it's more than that," M.N. said. "After all, Sally Ann is white. She would feel one way, but E.A. would have to feel something else. It's a lot worse for him."

"Maybe he didn't think about that, though," I hoped. "*We* never talked about it with him."

"No, we didn't. Do you think maybe we should have?"

"I guess there'll be lots of times when he'll have to think about it himself," I said. "Or when people will make him think about it. You can bet somebody like Tommy Ditford or Fats Browning would mention it soon enough."

"They'd do more than that," M.N. said.

I agreed.

"It will take a lot of time," said Mother, standing in the doorway, "for people not to see the black outside before they see the person inside."

24

We both looked up as Mother came in and sat on the bed with M.N.

"You don't mind if I just sit here a while with you, do you?" she said. And then, after a minute of silence, she said, "You know, there are a lot of things we haven't talked about, things that have happened. And some that haven't."

"We know," M.N. said.

"We may never talk about them, some of them," Mother said.

I thought a minute. "That doesn't mean we haven't thought about them, though."

"You're right, Michael," Mother said. "It's funny, isn't it? In a way, M.N. here and your father are closer than before. They understand each other better. They're kinder than they were. And neither has really said that much to the other."

"I thought it would be better to show things, rather than to talk about them," M.N. said. "I mean, there are some things you just can't talk about."

"I know. You're right to do things your own way," agreed Mother. "As long as it's the way you truly feel. You've given us a lot to think about, M.N."

"Yes, I know," M.N. said, very low.

"But it's not entirely your fault, dear," Mother went on. "There are things each of us should have known about the other."

"But *you* weren't wrong, Mother!" M.N. said quickly. "It should have worked out. It all should have."

"I think so, too," Mother said. "I just wish we could start all over again, and live these past months a lot differently, and better."

"Could they have been that much different?" I asked.

"Could they?" Mother asked me in turn.

"Yes," I said finally. "I guess so."

"Michael," Mother said, "M.N. and your father have made a sort of peace now. Isn't it your turn?"

"How do you mean?" I asked.

Mother thought a minute, as though she were trying different words out in her mind. "I mean," she said at last, "that none of us can afford to judge the other too harshly."

"I'm not judging anyone," I said.

"Yes, you are," Mother answered. "I'm not sure I blame you, really. But sometimes what worries your father are bigger problems than those we ourselves have."

"But they're exactly the same size," M.N. said. "After all, Father himself says we should consider everyone, not just those closest to us."

"Yes," Mother said. "But sometimes there is a difference between what one says and what one does."

"There shouldn't be!" I said, sort of deep. "There shouldn't be any differences at all if what Father says is right."

"That's exactly what I mean, Michael," Mother told me, "about being too harsh a judge."

No one said anything then, for a minute. Finally, Mother stood up and moved towards the door of my room. "Michael," she said, "when Sally Ann and your father came back from their walk the other day, he said to me that he wished *you* had gone with them. He misses his walks with you, you know."

I started to say that if that were true, it was his own fault. But I stopped.

"The important thing, Michael," Mother said, "is not always to understand your father, but to remember that he *is* your father. Even if what he does seems strange to you, or wrong, if you love him at all you don't stop letting him know it."

And as she turned to leave, Mother added: "If you *can* understand later, that's wonderful, too, of course."

Then she left.

25

I haven't talked much about how I feel towards Father now. It isn't easy, really, is why. One day I feel one thing, and the next something different altogether.

But I didn't want to take one of our walks. I didn't want to have to talk alone with him. I was glad he was busy at the church, and all I really wanted was to be left alone, with M.N. or my books or something, until I figured out what I figured out.

The thing is, if you decide to do something, then you do it. You can't change your mind all the time.

Maybe that's too simple. What I mean is that if you want E.A., then you want him. You have to worry about a lot of stuff, of course, but these worries have to come after you worry about *him*. At least, they would with me.

I think people would have gotten used to E.A. after a while. They might even have forgotten about him some time. After all, they've got other things to do, too, besides complain about one little kid.

And if people can forget, so could Father's church. If Father had stood up the way he was always telling us to do, people would have had to say something like, "Well, maybe I don't quite understand him, but I've got to admire him anyway."

That would have done it, I think. That word, admire. If Mother can tell me it isn't always as important to understand someone as it is to stand beside them when they're in trouble—which is what, I figure, she was really saying— then the same thing would go for other people, too. They didn't have to understand Father as long as they could count on him.

And that, you see, is what I couldn't do any more. Count on him. He had told me what was important, and what wasn't, and then he went ahead and mixed them up. And everything that happened to us and to E.A. happened just because he did get them mixed up.

M.N. would have made her own kind of deal with herself about E.A. in time. The parents of the church school kids would, too, because they would have to: it's probably the best school around. And it's easy to find a grocery store for shopping. The cross, of course, is something else. But as M.N. said to me once, how many nights can you stay up late just to strike a match?

So you can see why I didn't want to walk with Father. At least, not yet.

Naturally, I had to. The very next day. He just came up and asked me. I couldn't have said no. I just couldn't have.

26

It was late afternoon. We walked down the path and turned right on our usual route. Father held his pipe in one hand and had the other stuck in his pocket.

I couldn't help myself. Prince Philip was walking on Father's right.

We didn't talk at all for a while. We just kept walking, past the big houses, through the shadows of eucalyptus trees, past the few cars parked along the curb. I wasn't going to say anything first. I felt it was up to Father.

He must have guessed I didn't feel much like helping, for finally he said, "Well, Michael, we haven't talked in quite some time, have we?"

"No," I allowed.

"Why is that? Aren't we friends any more?"

"I don't know. There doesn't seem to be much worth talking about," I said.

"Do you really believe that?" Father asked.

"No, I don't. But there isn't much I *want* to talk about."

"You're a stern judge, Michael."

"Mother said the same thing. But I'm fair, too."

"How?" Father asked. "How are you fair, when you won't even hear my case?"

"You don't have a case! After all you've told us, and *everything,* you went right ahead and ruined it all at once."

"That wasn't my intention."

"That doesn't make any difference to me!" I said fast, rushing on in spite of myself, wanting more to listen but having for some reason to talk instead. "You let everyone else get in the way of what you wanted to do, of what you knew was right. You let the church and the school, and Mary Nell, get between you and what you planned. You backed down!"

"Ah, Michael," Father started to say, but I wasn't finished.

"You can't possibly be a whole man. You want to live different parts of your life differently, and that's not right. *You* taught me that. And whether you like it or not, I still want to believe in it."

Father walked in silence for a minute. "Perhaps someday—not now, but in a year or so, Michael, you *will* let me present my case. Perhaps with a little more time, things won't seem quite so simple. It's hard to see everything when you're twelve."

I didn't say anything. A year is a very long time.

"But other people," Father said, "and what they said and wanted did get to my weakest spot. To give in seemed to be the easiest thing to do. For a moment, even, it seemed the right thing to do. And in that moment, I did let you down, Michael. I let everyone down. I'm sorry for that, truly. Just as I was sorry the minute I drove away from the adoption agency."

"That was one minute too late!" I snapped.

I was sorry, as soon as I heard it, that I had said what I said in just the way I said it. But it was true, and there wasn't anything to do about it.

We walked a little farther, then, without talking. A light breeze was coming in from the ocean and you could just begin to see the afternoon fog falling from the hills. We passed a huge house where there was an opera on the phonograph, playing very loudly, and you could hear someone singing along with parts of it.

"You'll be glad to know," Father said then, very slowly, "that the church feels pretty much the same way you do, Michael."

"About what?"

"About me, and what has happened."

"What do you mean?" I asked.

"I mean that even though we gave E.A. back as the board asked, they still aren't happy. They're as disappointed in me as you are. In fact, they've asked me to look for another parish."

I looked up at Father. He had a sort of sad smile on his face as he looked at me, and he shook his head a little. "You see, there are just deserts, after all, aren't there?"

"But that's awful!" I said. "How can they do that? You only did what they wanted in the first place."

"That's true, but apparently they feel I should have stood up to them, had the courage to follow through what I had begun, regardless. They would have respected me more, they say, if I had."

I didn't say anything. I was too surprised.

"You know, Michael, it's a funny thing. Sometimes people haven't got the strength themselves to do what they know they ought to. They need help. They need a leader. But when they find one, they still aren't happy. They expect more and more, and the minute a leader thinks he's finally gotten everything solved, and done, the people find something else still to be unhappy with. Like Moses in the desert. He and the Lord worked very hard to make life easier for their people, but the people still weren't—"

"*Why*," I interrupted, angry again, "*why* do you have to talk about that sort of stuff? What about what's happened *here,* at home? What about Mother, or Sally Ann, or E.A.? What about him? What has this all done to *him?*" I had *tried* not to think about E.A., but it's hard, late at night, when you're alone, to always just think about what you want to.

"I've thought of all that," Father said slowly. "Michael, I *have* thought about those things."

"You should have thought *before*, not after," I said.

"I did, Michael," said Father. "Before and after. But I *knew* more afterwards."

"Yes, when it was too late!"

"Is it too late, Michael? Is it too late, do you think?"

"Don't *you* think so?" I asked right back.

"Yes, I guess I do," Father said. "But I still hope it's not too late to fix some things."

"Well," I said, a little softer now, "I don't see how you could have done much worse than you did. You must have learned *some*thing."

"You *are* harsh, Michael."

"No more so than Mother," I said, without knowing really why I thought that.

"Perhaps not. She feels we should have been more determined. We should have faced the town and the church and M.N., too, and done exactly as we had planned."

"What do you think?" I asked, holding my breath.

"I agree, Michael. I agree."

We crossed a street into the last of the day's sunlight.

"What are you going to do now?" I asked Father.

"Resign, I think. I want to," he said.

"Then what happens?"

"Then," Father said, "I guess we start all over again."

I thought about this. "Good. I think that's good," I said. "I'll miss some of the things we have here, but I'll be glad to go somewhere else."

"Because of what's happened?" Father asked.

"Yes, I guess so," I said.

"If I felt there were a way to stay," Father said, "and do something good with the time left us, we would have to stay."

"But there isn't, is there?" I asked. "I mean, what's happened has happened, and that's that. You can't start over again here."

"Do you think we should try to get Edgar Allan back and take him with us?" Father asked suddenly.

I hadn't ever even thought about this. I did then, but just for a minute. "Has he found another family? I mean, has someone else adopted him now?"

Father nodded yes.

"Then, no," I said. "I don't think so. It's better to let him stay where he is. Better than having him given away again."

Father nodded. "But when we get to wherever we're going next, maybe we could take another child, and start him properly, *really*. No backing down, no changing our minds, no weakening at the last minute."

"Is there another way we could do some good?" I asked Father then. "Because if there is, let's do that, instead. At least, for a while."

"You still don't quite trust me, do you?"

I wanted very much to say yes. "No," I said, sort of quiet.

"That's all right, Michael," Father said, putting his hand on my shoulder. "Maybe there's more I have to learn about being both a man and a minister, and about how they go together."

We stopped walking then, and just looked at each other. "You know something?" I said.

"What?"

"How come your sermon last week was so short?"

"Oh, Michael!" Father said with a smile. "Nothing ever escapes you, does it? It was short because I no longer felt I had the right to talk to people in the same way I used to. There wasn't much I could say from up there that made sense to me any more. Not that I doubted God, Michael. I suddenly doubted man. I doubted me."

"Do you still?" I asked.

"As long as I have *all* of you, no. No."

"That's good," I said. "Because if M.N. can change, I don't see why the rest of the world can't."

So we turned around and walked home, through the twilight. And I saw the year's first falling leaves.